An I Can Read Book™

Minnie and Moo
The Attack of
the Easter Bunnies

Den s Cazet

HarperCollins*Publishers*

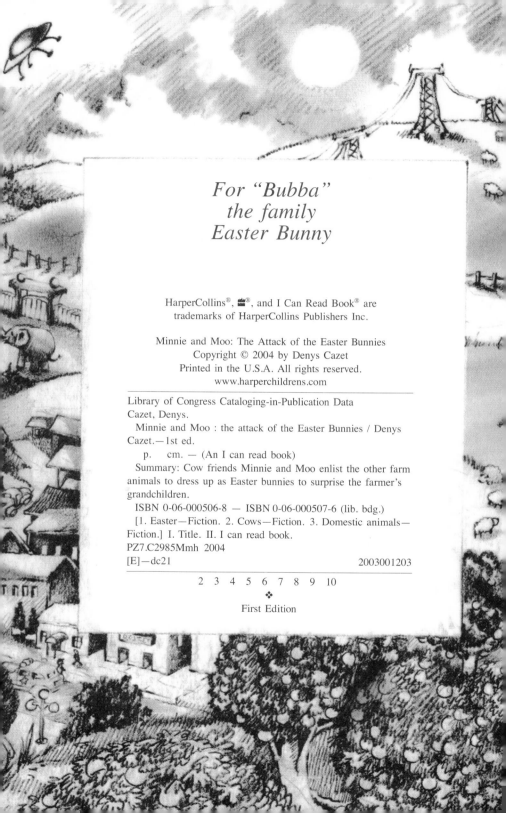

For "Bubba"
the family
Easter Bunny

HarperCollins®, 🏭®, and I Can Read Book® are
trademarks of HarperCollins Publishers Inc.

Minnie and Moo: The Attack of the Easter Bunnies
Copyright © 2004 by Denys Cazet
Printed in the U.S.A. All rights reserved.
www.harperchildrens.com

Library of Congress Cataloging-in-Publication Data
Cazet, Denys.
  Minnie and Moo : the attack of the Easter Bunnies / Denys
Cazet.—1st ed.
    p.   cm. — (An I can read book)
  Summary: Cow friends Minnie and Moo enlist the other farm
animals to dress up as Easter bunnies to surprise the farmer's
grandchildren.
  ISBN 0-06-000506-8 — ISBN 0-06-000507-6 (lib. bdg.)
  [1. Easter—Fiction. 2. Cows—Fiction. 3. Domestic animals—
Fiction.] I. Title. II. I can read book.
PZ7.C2985Mmh 2004
[E]—dc21   2003001203

2 3 4 5 6 7 8 9 10
❖
First Edition

No Easter Bunny?

Minnie snoozed

under the old oak tree.

Moo colored Easter eggs.

"Almost ready," she said.

Minnie opened one eye.

"Why bother?" she said.

"The Easter Bunny isn't coming."

"What?" Moo gasped. "Minnie!

How can you say such a thing?"

"Don't blame me," said Minnie.

"Blame the farmer.

He told Mrs. Farmer he was too old

to be the Easter Bunny."

"But, Minnie!" said Moo.

"His grandchildren are coming.

Who will be the Easter Bunny?"

"Don't look at me," said Minnie.

Moo looked at Minnie.

"Moo, I'm too big!" Minnie said.
"Who ever heard of an Easter Bunny
as big as a cow?"

"Who, then?" Moo asked.

Minnie pointed at the chicken coop.

"Elvis," she said.

The Easter Rooster

Elvis was lying on a table.

A chicken named Gina

rubbed his feet.

When Elvis saw Minnie and Moo

he pulled a towel over his head.

"I'm not here!" he said.

"I went to South America."

"The farmer says he's too old
to be the Easter Bunny," said Moo.
"Don't you cows listen?" said Elvis.
"I just told you I wasn't here!"
"We want you to be
the Easter Bunny," said Minnie.

"HA!" said Elvis. "Me?"

"Please?" said Moo.

"Go away," said Elvis.

"Help them," said Gina.

"Help the children."

"I'm busy," said Elvis.

"Then so am I!" said Gina.

She went into the hen house

and slammed the door.

"Now you did it!" said Elvis.

"Doesn't anyone ever think of me?"

"But—" said Moo.

"No!" said Elvis. "Try the pigs."

3

The Easter Pig

The pigs were soaking in the mud.

"Can you help us?" Moo asked.

"We need someone to dress up

as the Easter Bunny."

One of the pigs grunted.

Another pig burped.

"I'll do it," said a small pig.

"Who said that?" Minnie asked.

"Over here," said the small pig.

"It's me, Hamlet."

Hamlet put his book down.

14

"I have to ask my mom first."

They looked into the mud hole.

"Which one is your mother?"

asked Minnie.

"She's in there somewhere,"
said Hamlet. "They all look alike."
"While you're looking," said Moo,
"we'll go ask the sheep."

4

The Easter Sheep

Minnie and Moo stood

in the middle of the sheep.

"So," said Moo. "Will you help us?"

"I don't know," said a sheep.

"Would we have to hop?"

"Hop?" said Minnie.

"Sheep shouldn't hop," said another.

All the sheep nodded.

"We could frisk," said one.

"Frisking is okay, but no hopping."

"Please!" said Moo.

"Is it okay with the farmer?" asked a big sheep.

"How about Mrs. Farmer?"

"Or the dog?" asked another.

"The dog?" said Minnie.

"He's the boss," said a sheep.

"Can't you make up

your own minds?" Minnie asked.

"Well, yes," said another sheep.

"And no," said another.

"Sometimes," said one.

"Maybe," said the big sheep.

"Come on, Moo," said Minnie.

5

The Easter Turkey

"There are Zeke and Zack," said Moo.

She told the turkeys about

the farmer and the Easter Bunny.

"So," she said. "Will you help us?"

Zeke looked at Zack.

Zack looked at Zeke.

"What's an Easter Bunny?" Zack asked.

"Beats me," said Zeke.

Minnie rolled her eyes.

"The Easter Bunny," said Moo,

"brings colored eggs to children."

"Why?" asked Zeke.

"It's a kind of spring party

for the new year," said Moo.

"The egg is a sign of new life."

Zeke looked at Zack.

"I'll be darned. Did you know that?"

"I didn't even know

bunnies laid eggs," said Zack.

6

The Easter Cow

"That does it!" said Minnie.

She marched off toward the barn.

"Minnie, wait," cried Moo.

"Where are you going?"

Minnie threw open the barn door

and stomped inside.

She opened an old trunk.

"Minnie, what are you doing?"
asked Moo.

"Moo," said Minnie, "if no one
will help us, we'll do it ourselves!"
Minnie pulled out two bunny suits
and held them up.

"Good," she muttered. "Extra large!"

"But, Minnie," said Moo. "You said
cows were too big to be—"

"There's no one left to help us!"
said Minnie.

Minnie put her arm around Moo.

"Besides, there's something even better

than one big Easter Bunny

at an Easter party."

"What?" asked Moo.

"Two big Easter Bunnies,"

said Minnie. "Come on!"

7

The Easter Bunnies

Minnie and Moo hid the Easter eggs in the farmer's backyard.

"There," said Moo.

"Now let's hide in the tool shed. After the children find all the eggs, we'll hop out and surprise them."

"Here they come," said Minnie.

Minnie and Moo ran into the shed.

"It's dark in here," said Moo.

"Scary dark," said a voice.

"Who's there?" Minnie asked.

"It's us, the sheep," said the sheep.

"We're here, next to Zeke and Zack."

"Yep," said Zeke.

"Yep," said Zack.

"Ouch!" cried Elvis. "Watch where you're stepping, you little pig."

"Oh, sorry," said Hamlet.

"Hamlet?" said Moo.

"My mom said it was okay!" he said.

"Elvis?" said Minnie.

"Yeah, yeah," said Elvis. "I'm here.

Thanks to you the chickens

won't let me in the coop

unless I help!"

Moo peeked out the dusty window.

"Here comes the farmer!" she said.

"He knows!" said one of the sheep.

"The dog told on us!"

"Quiet," Minnie said.

8

Attack of the Easter Bunnies

The farmer opened the door.

"Where did I hang that old

Easter Bunny suit?" he grumbled.

He turned on the light.

"BAAAAAAAAA!" shouted the sheep.

"AHHHHHHHHH!" shouted the farmer.

He ran out the door.

"Save the children!" the farmer cried.

"Giant rabbits in the tool shed!"

"What's all the shouting about?"
said Mrs. Farmer.
"Attack of the Easter Bunnies!"
gasped the farmer.

"Easter Bunnies?" said Mrs. Farmer.

"Easter Bunnies?" said the children.

"Look! Here they come!"

The sheep ran out of the tool shed.

"Frisk!" Moo yelled. "Frisk!"

Moo pointed at Elvis. "Go!"

"I'm going," said Elvis.

"But I'm not frisking."

Elvis strutted down the hill.

"My turn," said Hamlet.

He hopped into the yard

and did some fancy piggy steps.

Zeke and Zack hopped into the yard

and pretended to lay an egg.

"Hooray!" cheered the children.

"It's an Easter parade!"

Minnie and Moo danced
around the children.
The children danced
around Minnie and Moo.

Minnie and Moo waved good-bye

and hopped over the garden fence.

The farmer's wife put her arm
around the farmer.

"Now I see why you didn't wear
the bunny suit," she whispered.
"You had this all planned."

"Well, I . . ." said the farmer.

The children hugged him.

"Thank you, Grandpa," they said.

"Well, I . . ." he said.

Mrs. Farmer kissed his cheek.

"Happy Easter," she said.

"Happy Easter," said the children.

The farmer scratched his head.

"Well . . . Happy Easter," he said.